The Gen-Y POET

J. Valentine

The Gen-Y POET

J. Valentine

pblishing.com
write • share • connect • publish

The **Gen-Y** POET by J. Valentine

Published in 2017 by www.pblishing.com

pblishing.com
write · share · connect · publish

Marketed by

Maple Press Private Limited
Sales Office A 63, Sector 58, Noida 201 301, U.P., India
phone +91 120 455 3581, 455 3583
email info@**maple**press.co.in
website www.**maple**press.co.in

ISBN: 978-81-93324-89-9

Cover and Book Design by Flying Trees Private Limited
Printed at Yash Printographics, Noida

10 9 8 7 6 5 4 3 2 1

Acknowledgement

I would like to thank my family, without whom none of this would have been possible, and in particular my parents, who have demonstrated preposterous patience in dealing with me over the years. Everything I will ever write is only because of the two of you.

That is a debt I will never be able to repay.

Contents

A SHIELD OF DREAMS

I can fly over mountains
fight wars for freedom
play God in my head
with no rhyme or reason
I can fill oceans with blood
bring a turn in seasons
but I can't control what happens
when I finally awaken

Treasure do I those moments
where I have complete control
when only I dictate the happenings
of the world I adore
I write the script
the plot twists are all known
but it ends with the dream
no matter how hard I wish for it to drag on

Reality is a double edged sword
unmerciful and cruel
dreams are but solid shields
to protect: stand the viscous blows
without them I would crumble
to the fear of life and love
just another unruly victim
of reality and life's limbo

The fates dictate all
we have no say
dreams can not stop them
we are bound to obey
the little control given
snatched at the light of day
just enough to keep us content...
God's perfect, little men.

ANGEL OF LIFE

She skips joyously
in a clean, white gown;
so beautiful is her soul
it lights her face to shine out.
Never have I witnessed
such untempered grace;
beloved is this angel,
she must be kept safe.

The very essence of life
flows through her clear veins;
Purity incarnate,
the beating heart of humanity.
She couldn't be more simple
not an imperfection to be seen.
Oh this angel is a dear,
so full of life and good things.

Her footsteps create saplings,
a touch sprouts flowers in-bloom.
She can not be tamed
free as the wild winds;
the Angel of Life answers to none
but loves us all the same.
We were born at her hand,
but die by another's blade.

I heard her singing softly
warm and loving a tune,
to a mouse at death's brink
she could not help but look gloom.
Her sad tears fell quiet
at the small body in her hands.
As it took its last breath,
she broke down in great pain.

Imagine her plight,
the gift that can only give.
She has no control,
cannot interfere with the mistress' course.
Loving all her creations,
losing a part of herself,
the Angel of Life
is destined to die everyday.

BLISS

I found bliss
away from humanity;
surrounded by soothing sea,
waves a gentle lullaby to me.
I could fall asleep,
drift away, content;
pray I should be so lucky
to feel this peace again.

I found bliss
away from humanity;
surrounded by birds
chirping merry melodies.
I could stay with them,
lose myself in this gentle tune;
never meet another soul
die cradled in nature's womb.

I found bliss
away from humanity;
the dance of fleeting fishes,
a hypnotic sight to behold in.
There they reveal
the mystery of life:
let the world turn as it may
being happy is but a state of mind.

I found bliss
but I must wake up much too soon;
for all I can do is dream
to be free from my cruel bones.
I have to go back...
I must return home.
But I promise to take this bliss
and change the world.

CLIMATIC GENOCIDE

We've changed the world
but don't rejoice and celebrate...
it's true we've changed the world
but by ruining it completely.

Striding into our "birthright"
with humanity's arrogant swagger
taking more than we ever needed
exhausting what sustained magical millennia.

If that wasn't bad enough
we've only polluted all that remained.
Toxic filth spewed everywhere
repeated again and again, day after day.

There's no pride to be felt
as the ice caps sinfully melt.
No purity left in the air
we've tainted every breathable layer.

It's hot where it was cold,
it snows in deserts now,
the tides have dangerously risen,
yet we continue to be unshaken.

We've destroyed the world in our madness
damaged mother earth beyond repair

History will sadly chuckle
at how we ultimately ruined ourselves.

As species of wildlife wither away,
dead at our hands: ego's prey.
How much longer can we continue to justify
this sustained climatic genocide?

As nature strikes back to stop our mad march,
tsunamis and earthquakes wipe innocent numbers in half.
Is this a war we wish to be in?
Is not our defeat blatantly clear?

Think about it for a second,
let the consequences sink in.
We get only one mother
to either cherish or to maim.

Care for her deeply
don't let another artic cap break away, please
this climatic genocide is self-mutilation
we need collective effort, not just solitary endeavours.

COSMIC CANCER

Are we cosmic cancer
here to taint the universe?
This ever growing organism,
are we only here to kill it?

A vast unknown
the skies above.
Are we poisoning it slowly?
Killing it from the inside out?

Makers of our own destiny
forging the paths we trod upon
always meant to be in control,
it can't all be a lie... can it?

What if every coincidence is scripted?
Random chance a farce?
If everything you do is written
free will goes for a toss.

'The universe doesn't exist,
it's not alive to begin with'
We haven't even explored our system,
there are galaxies unknown to us.

So there may yet exist
a heart to this universe

it may well and truly live–
this 'God' you so adore.

Only to die at our hand.
How tragic would that be?
Don't forget that if the universe dies...
so must we.

We might well be cosmic cancer
but we can still save our souls.
If we don't stop this sustained destruction,
there may not be a tomorrow to repent for.

Of course we're cosmic cancer
we care not for our wondrous world.
Maybe we are meant to realise too late
left doomed in our folly fate.

FINDING FRIENDSHIP

My mother always said,
'Your friends are too old.
Why don't you have any
closer to your own?'
She always thought
that age defined friendship;
she always assumed
t'was a prerequisite.

On the first day of school
my teacher screeched aloud,
'Don't sit with the girls,
the boys sit over there!'
She always thought
that gender defined friendship;
she always assumed
there was no other way.

As we grew older
my friends insisted,
'Stay away from the geeks,
the jocks sit over here.'
They always thought
that labels defined friendships;
they always assumed
the different cannot intermix.

When I became a father
my daughter asked me once,
'Daddy, I made a new friend,
can I bring her in to play now?'
The help's little daughter,
they walked hand in hand.
All she cared about
was the heart beating within.

They say friendships are fleet,
unreliable, and utopian,
the world is harsh
every man only his own.
But they do forget
that the empathy of a good friend
along with his loyalty
can make mice into men.

So now if someone asks me
I always say the same thing.
I truly believe there is magic
somethings are beyond our experiences.
There is no reason in the world
why friendship can't be eternal,
through many a lives,
a whole.

FIRES OF ANGER

Anger has no restraints,
no limits, no chains,
can you craft shackles
that can tame its fiery rage?

Words won't help
when you're free-falling down this rabbit hole.
They hold no power over me,
these daily playthings of mine you speak

What can anyone do to show
that this reaction is unnecessary?
How can anyone prove
that the way you feel won't last eternity?

Everyone has the freedom
to feel what they want;
no one can tell you it's wrong,
they're your choices to drown in after all

So get angry
but only for what's unjustifiably wrong.
Follow it through to the very end
no matter how many bridges you must burn.

We're angry,
this fire, it's scorching hot.

It'll lay waste to everything...
even what you truly hold dear.

This anger–
be wary, it'll burn your life up
only let it roam free
if you can brave the fallout.

GANGSTERS OF LOVE

There are those who roam
pillage through our world,
caring not for their bodies
but the deeds of their souls.
They might not be normal
but can't be made to adhere;
a gang of broken souls
unimaginably feared.

They want not your flattery
nor will they cower at contempt;
care not for folly things
no time for the inconvenient.
Much more on their minds
deeds aplenty to be done still,
some may not be angels
but all soldiers must sin.

They arrive like a hurricane
ruthless and swift.
Such is their fabled strength
even regimes known to wilt.
It may take a day
or a millennia at best,
but these gangsters are infamous
for their iron will and zest.

No one can buy them off
incorruptible to the bone;
their solitary wish
is to change our whole world.
Don't write them off too soon
doubting them a grave error;
these gangsters are known
for their unwavering valour.

Gargantuan in number
united in their diversity.
So much love for the world
a trigger for any just triviality.
Imagine then the power
behind every great cause.
These gangsters will ever gather
to fight all righteous wars.

They will knock on your door,
break it down if they must.
Roaring like lions
they'll take what you owe.
Unmerciful towards hate
demanding their just dues
these gangster can be cruel
when debts are left to accrue.

Your cosmic debt deep
life is an expensive affair.
This debt is unpayable

and yet, somehow, you must pay it.
It only asks that you treat
all life with utmost respect;
stop the perpetual persecution,
stop this bloody mess.

Their battlecry is simple–
'Love To All.'
The message quite clear:
Please put down your arms.
They couldn't care less
about caste, colour, creed
the Gangsters of Love
only want eternal peace.

Love is beast to behold,
caging it a mortal sin,
neither time nor tide,
can cut its rainbow wings.
Armed with pistols of peace
and ammunition of acceptance,
the Gangsters of Love
are immortal in essence.

HUMAN NATURE

Behold the beauty of nature
mirrored in the minds of men
these constants of human life
unabating till our last blink.

We are subject to the same instincts
food, safety, and security do we crave
never ending are our wants and desires
while we wait for death's gentle embrace.

To sloth, gluttony and greed we cave
to pride and lust we fall
envy and wrath are not too far behind
to make us drop to our knees and bow.

Everyone is opportunistic
each seeking their own gains
by pen, thought, or sword we strike all down
who dare block paths to claim coveted crowns.

Love do we all seek
hoping to complete our soul
they say Gods made us a part of a whole
cursed on a quest to fill this empty hole.

Life will forever move
for nature waits for no one and listens to less

in our control is barely enough
to live with little regret.

LAST SLICE OF BREAD

I stumbled across a bakery
the fumes within entice me;
a child of four
drawn to the smell of flour.
Hunger growls vicious
my hands begin to tremble
a tear slips down my cheek
as I watch and cry in pain,
the last slice of bread
thrown out once again.

I grow older still
but no escape in sight,
this wretched place,
that forsaken bakery
with lust I look upon
my heart weeps in anguish;
a part of me dies
barely holding in the scream...
as the last slice of bread
is fed to the dirt over me.

I look at my children now,
a distraught sight
for everyday I must witness
a part of them too die.
Some lucky days

meagre food on the plate,
most days we cry
sleeping hungry in one bed,
and all I can think about
is that last slice of bread wasted again.

I start my demise
lay light on my death bed,
the doctor spouts words
'malnourished' and 'deficient'
I close my eyes
and wonder if hunger will follow me,
with my last breath I say,
'Don't worry, don't cry,
maybe heaven is the place
where those slices of bread I shall finally find.'

MOTHER EARTH'S LOVER

The winds rustle them leaves
a melody millennia old
soft, gentle breeze
sends shivers through my soul.
Quiet serenity in this blazing world
a moment's peace is unheard of
lost is this eternal trance
replaced by charmless chaos untold.

If death can even mimic
this bliss of old
it's easy to see the appeal,
the longing, the want
a place untouched by evils
living with nature in harmony
alone with the devil himself
embracing eternal ecstasy.

They say loneliness breeds
in silent surroundings
peace can not last forever
minds of men fickle fields.
But the seeds that blossom in chaos
unable to do so in the serene?
The seeds that break through hate
incapable of growing in peace?

The world is unyielding
cruel is our dystopic peace.
Harmony unable to foster
a better world lay forgotten beneath.
The essence of life lost
left behind in a race for pleasures
empty hope is all that remains
to inspire a heard of mechanical cattle.

Green cover ablaze
a sea of ash and blood
if you've forgotten your love for the world
try and remember how much you need her.
Serene surroundings scotched
nothing left to salvage anymore
for material possessions make up
the soul of humanity, dear lord.

When nature ripped away
from the cradle of Mother Earth
her bloodlust for revenge
will be a sight to behold.
The day Mother Earth
must wail for her life
mankind will be lost
forever in her pride.

MISTRESS OF DEATH

Bring out the drums,
let the children play;
it's time to let live
and time to obey.
We are all subjects
to the Mistress of Death;
sometimes she feels lenient,
sometimes, hell bent.

She stands gracefully
in a black silken gown;
the most beautiful woman
to ever be frowned upon.
Her eyes look tired,
the sparkle within gone,
maybe it's time she stopped
picking up souls at dawn.

Can one even comprehend
the toll that it takes?
Tearing families apart
and coming back for the rest.
She feels bogged down
tired of all the pain,
it's time for the Mistress
to think about retiring again.

But she has to go on
no luxury of choice,
immortality is a privilege
not bestowed upon all.
Only Gods do not fall
for the Mistress' charm
but for all mortal men
one day she will come.

PARADOXES OF HUMAN PLIGHT

Every breath you need
you're as young as you will ever be
and as old as you will ever feel
simultaneous paradoxes of human plight this be.

You'll never know tomorrow
can't rewrite yesterday
only left with the present
whatever shall you make of it?

That's the only question, you see
that you must ask constantly
the only time that truly matters
is when you're awake to do your deeds.

So be, do be,
be all that you want to be.
Just be it in the now
there's never a tomorrow for these things.

These are, these are, these are
the paradoxes of human plight, you see
this false sense of security
is a trap for the wavering.

These are, these are, these are
the paradoxes of human plight, you see

some things in life
we are all meant to feel.

STARS OF HUMANITY

These small little stars shine
like little peep holes
the Gods above spying
upon their lowly clones.
We are but their entertainment–
secret little puppet shows
to be looked at from afar
admired but never dotted upon.

These small little stars shine
a symbol of empty hope
maybe someday, somehow
Gods may decide to show.
They let us believe
that we are not alone
as the world is cruelly crumbling
God's mercy shall be a sight to behold.

These small little stars shine
to show the unknown universe
we are but slowly dying
at no ones hand but our own.
If the Gods made all
the entirety of life
how can they be so bashfully blind
to human suffering and strife?

These small little stars shine
rhythmic heartbeat to us below.
If there is indeed life out there
I beg you to stop us yet.
All the rape, murder, mayhem,
the systematic killing of innocents–
Is this not enough to shock our souls?
Are we not worth more than sacrificial sport?

These small little stars shine
mocking us from above
laughing at the absurdities
that we are capable of.
How have we managed to sink so low?
Unrecognisably lost to our very own souls?
And yet these Gods watch quiet
all this misery merely scripted drama for a fool?

These small little stars shine
as I arrive at the same destitute end:
maybe no help is coming
maybe we truly are beyond repair.
The Gods have truly given up
their hearts crushed in despair;
there may be no hope at all...
until we make some for ourselves.

These small little stars shine
shedding light on our past deeds;
We are so much more

than all that we have been.
The time has come
to stand up for our sakes
how can anyone help us
until we learn to help ourselves?

SEDITIOUS SENSELESSNESS

We live in a world
shrouded in terror;
protected by men
of unimaginable valour.
They ask for nothing
yet we somehow do less;
how mighty of us
to betray their trust.

Speak out against the government,
criticise till you cry shrill;
but know the difference
between politics and nation.
We elect mortal men
though our nation a wonder immortal;
throw the unworthy away
but speak no ill of our mother.

Brave blood gushed in rivers
to shape this land of ours;
no doubts or disagreements
over their sacrifices for this just cause.
The ashes of our founders
lie ashamed and in pain;
lives laid down for the nation
not for the men who would run it.

Every act of sedition
a slap on their faces;
tainting their achievements,
rubbishing their accolades.
Every act of sedition
must be answered in kind;
we owe them our freedom,
how can we turn blind eyes?

Democracy demands dissent,
it even craves for healthy debate;
but what it can never condone
is disrespecting the nation.
Sedition seduces spineless men to sin
though flippant use its equally thoughtless twin.
Freedom to be truly felt
can never be unrestrictedly unlimited.

If there are no boundaries
how will we ever comprehend
the concrete certainty in our actions,
or the morbid morality in just sanctions?
We will never know the power
that great liberty bestows;
fight over meanings and nuances
not over the mother in whom you grow.

Sedition is but a matricidal snare,
spits on the graves of our noble dead;
remember who fights for this nation–

every selfless soldier in unappreciated creation.
Never a shield to be used
against tiny, trivial acts
but a necessary sword
restrictively used to just jab.

We must be united,
do not be led astray;
how dare you break the hearts
of the valiant who died for this day?
Turn away from seditious senselessness,
do not stand with the wilfully wrong.
This ungrateful insurgency is unforgivable,
our martyrs demand a greater due.

Sedition is not some lowly crime,
wretched and utterly vile.
A myriad of fallen souls didn't die
for this blatant abuse of our God-given rights.
Be proud of your country,
bask bold in its glorious history,
protect until your last breath
our mother's sacred dignity.

THE STAGE OF LIFE

Do what you do
but only what you love to do
I'm begging you to do it
there are billions waiting for you.

We're holding our breath
hoping your quest bears righteous fruit.
Oh to be basking in your glory
would fill us with joy to our roots.

The stage of life,
it's been waiting for you,
calling out your name,
beckoning for you to bloom.

I want to see the happiness
feel that pride glow within you,
take the colours that you need
paint a picture with every hue.

When you inevitably fall
rise higher than ever before,
grow with this journey
but always be better than your faults.

I'll just be flowing along
in my spring of eternal hope,

oh please, won't you please
just love what you do.

Don't leave it so late
that some of us miss out on you;
I've believed in you this long
but I don't have a forever to bet on you.

The stage of life,
it's ever begging for you,
do the best with what you're given,
the audience is ever willing.

The stage of life,
it's ever ready for you,
don't let all the hate
break that love blossoming within you.

THE FICTIONS OF FEAR

When you truly live
without ever feeling afraid
are you finally fearless
or merely camouflaging cowardice?

Is it possible to overcome
when you fail to feel?
Suppressing human emotions
is what truly makes us weak.

Fear is necessary,
bravery cannot exist without it;
breaking through barriers
is what's wondrous for warriors.

Don't bow to a man who feels no fear,
but kneel before the one who overcomes it;
don't listen to a person who boasts of bravery,
but learn from the one who silently performs it

Don't be in awe of those who never tremble,
but applaud the ones who overcome it;
don't beg before those who claim to teach valour
but learn from those who silently perform it

Be afraid, be terrified,
feel every nervous beat,

then do the right thing anyway
and let fictions of fear be fleet

Be hysterical, be petrified,
feel every bead of sweat
but always do the right thing
and let the fictions of fear be forgotten for today.

THOSE DAYS

It's one of those days
were everything goes wrong.
It starts when you awake
and your world keeps spiralling down.

Every step you walk
ends in a stumble,
every breath you take
only leaves you angrier.

It's one of those days
were nothing goes right.
No matter how hard you try
it must end in a cry.

Frustrated and hopeless,
everything overwhelms you;
drowning in this misery
that seems specially reserved for you.

And the worst part is
that these dreadful days
seem to stretch so long
that you'd do anything to end the pain.

It's just one of those days
the universe seems hell bent on your demise,

but I'll let you in on a secret–
everyone feels like that in life.

It's just one of those day
that you must overcome.
Who said life was easy?
There are tests you're meant to pass.

It's just one of those days
but it'll be over soon enough.
Just make sure you stay alive
for when it all works itself out.

WINDS OF CHANGE

Whistles and howls
these are my prouds
I was born before heaven
just let me get refreshened.

How do I know
what the universe has in store?
I've seen the grand plan
a solemn duty to perform.

I am the Winds of Change
such an inevitable bane
hated and berated
only to find you again.

For good or for bad,
for better or for worse,
whatever else may be
I will visit quite frequently.

Believe in me
or stay as stubborn as can be
but I know your strengths and your weaknesses,
I'm destined to find a way in.

You may have boarded doors
nailed windows shut, spewed lava on the floor.

Alas, I'm famed for my relentless drive,
there is nowhere for you to possibly hide.

My winds are rampant
how can you resist me?
Relentless and unwavering,
air must always find a way in.

I'd advise you to accept me
submission makes it so much easier.
Change is a perennial promise...
I'm only here to deliver it.

A THIEF'S APOLOGY

Stay away from me,
lock me and flee.
I'm a thief
a lowly cretin
throw away the key!
Forget where I be!

Close the door on me,
shut it hard.
A barricade must be
I need to steal
submit to the satisfaction
for the world to see.

I know where I went wrong,
it's not demonic desire or wicked want.
My cruel mind
digs deeper they said
the selfish satisfaction
of having what you dearly wanted.

I feed from it, see,
fills this darkness deep within me.
I'm of a miserable race
the bane of this world
we've done the most harm
but humanity we're ironically known.

But I get off point,
blabbering bits of bored beginnings.
Don't tell me I've done it again
stolen your heart oh so suddenly
I didn't mean to do it
I was just trying to be me.

I'm sorry for this thievery...
but is it really stealing
if it's only but a thoughtless deed?
I didn't mean for this to happen
you've gone and fallen for me.
I never even hoped to imagine that.

Have I drowned your light?
Stolen your sins for my nefarious needs?
How could I have let this happen!
I apologise for my mistakes
I don't know why it happened
there's just so much you refused to share.

Will you too shout now
explaining why I'm always in the wrong?
Throwing my faults right back at me
enjoying this manic bout of madness
I'll just sit there and take it
nothing can erase things once said.

So a jury must judge me,

scrutinise my intent,
peer into my mind's madness.
If they too pronounce me guilty
only then believe it.
Until then may I get the benefit?

I'm going to need it.
I'm a sucker for hearts after all,
I'm bound to steal again.

BUMBLEBEES

You hop like a bumblebee
buzzing free tree to tree
I pray you glance at me
so I may finally feel something.

You pop like a bumblebee
eagerly seeking nectar sweet
I'll gladly give you mine
if you'd consider me so worthy.

You stop like a bumblebee
at every sweet flower you see
I only hope to feel the glee
of someday watching you move towards me.

When the wind begins to bellow
you fly as far can be.
Whenever things get tough
will you forever feel this need to be free?

You seem lost in concrete jungles
buzzing blind in ravenous regret.
Begging for some help
afraid you're out of your depth.

What if I come for you then?
Will you finally fall for me?

Promises of a good life
are all I truly have to give.

What if I'm the beekeeper
here to tame you as my Queen?
Is that not enough,
am I so unworthy of your sting?

I'm sorry I'm the beekeeper...
Is that why you fiercely flee?
What if I catch you for my keep...
will you forever stay with me?

CUPID'S HEROIN

Your smiles are the subject
of romantic poems olde;
such seductive simplicity,
so sinfully soulful.
Every step you walk
holds heavenly grace
Gods left to wonder
if they must start staking claim.

Your glances akin to
sharp, steely swords;
clattering away madly
at the crumbling walls of my heart.
Every word you speak
so pure and right
hastily drowning out
the voices screaming inside.

Your eyes sparkle bright–
excited and free
wandering in search of
poor souls in need.
Your skin shimmers slight
so succulently sweet
to caress too long
induces insanity.

Every kiss of yours
leaves a celestial taste
addictive and sublime
a craving for all my days.
Every kiss of yours
blissful and pious
you must be Cupid's heroin,
because I'm blithely dying.

NORTH OF HEAVEN

I was tired of this insanity!
Our world made of vicious vanity.
Waiting for a piece of divine clarity,
begging for my forlorn ending charity!

I ran away on a whim
in a bout of rebellious naivety,
heard whispers from other worlds–
an impossible adventure of unspeakable rarity.

So I wrecked this frail body
pushed through torrents bloody
every second was excruciating
but we all endure necessary agony.

I know only where I must go
towards this fabled land, forgottenly old
there's no mysterious map to help
nor a soul to be found en route.

Only whispers of a vague promise
one which can never be enforced
yet its mere possibility
feeds my wanderlust of love.

This place somewhere near heaven
a love said to reside so true

they say it can mend what's broken
make it whole and true.

This place somewhere near heaven
a person said to live so pure
even Gods can not find faults
learn from the love that endlessly endures.

I pray to chance upon it someday
breathe the same air as this divine dame
if I'm ever as lucky as the number seven
to stumble across her land just North of Heaven.

ROMANTIC IMAGINATION

Sometimes I start to wonder,
wander deep into solitary oblivion;
peering at empty spaces,
lost to the ticks of time-keeping.

Enthralled by your allure:
heavenly, beautiful, and sublime;
lighting the dark descent back home,
only a Goddess could be so kind.

A script begins to unfurl,
a melody in infancy composed.
Of love and life and thoughts unbeknown,
our timeless tale so tenderly sewn.

Every greeting gets grander,
I'm captivated by every smile of yours;
covert glances leave my heart crumpled on the floor,
my romantic imagination starts running wild once more.

Old, hardened walls start to crumble,
guardsmen of my heart stand down;
for a nervy second I hear them mumble,
'This is it, old friend, you deserve a chance.'

As I get ready to take this leap of faith,
doubt sneaks in sudden to berate;

can we be impervious and unrattled
or does the incessant chatter of lost souls matter?

What happens if we should spectacularly fail?
Must we still push through a torrid tale?
And what happens if we don't compare
to the world I've dreamed about since we met?

These seeds grow into a raging storm
eating away at this perfect picture I've drawn;
rotting, corroding, stripping it bare,
destroying every hope I've ever held dear.

How could I deserve you,
when I barely deserve myself...
this doubt is unkind,
I feel myself giving in.

A nullifidian bowing to a Goddess,
a divine joke so ironically iniquitous;
oh how I wish we were impervious,
fear is the worst enemy from within.

Our unholy sin could not stand
somethings are not meant for this world;
Honey, you're every sweet dream I've ever dreamt
but I'm the nightmare you were born to loath.

I was shown the glaring flaw in our plan,
a drop of doubt shook our love so great:

Darling, you're made of the heavens above
but I'm a creature from hell underneath.

How could we partake in this parade,
dance to the drama of my mind's scripted charade?
You've roamed with angels in starry night skies
while I've nurtured my demons every damned day.

The universe rushes to stop our mortal sin,
tame this beast we've raised in lustful rebellion.
You grew up surrounded by good
while I was raised in my lonesome wicked woods.

This romantic imagination knows no bounds,
screaming young and free, boisterously proud.
I may understand why the universe crushed it so
but alas, hope can only be found on lost shores.

No two people could be as different,
as unknown to the other as us;
how I know this so very well,
but I couldn't help thinking of love.

This tale I've thought
I'm sorry I could not will it true.
You're too pious for my touch...
I couldn't damn you too.

What can I do now,
but tightly stitch my heart close?

Barricade myself again,
leave you with the others, out in the cold.

So I'm left alone again,
with only my romantic imagination to entertain;
wrestling with this innocent idea inane,
of letting you be my blissful bane.

SHRINES

In the cloudy night sky
I seek your shrine.
This temple divine
to claim as mine.

In the peaceful night sky
I search for your shrine.
Earth much too evil,
you're unknowingly kind.

In the blink of an eye
the skies start to pour.
I scoured the earth
only to be saved by your door.

In the dripping night sky
I knelt at your shrine.
The sins of my life
set right by your light.

In the moonlit night sky,
I preach your caring creed.
A devout believer
of this love so sweet.

In the eerie night sky
I practice your rites.

No sacrifice is ever enough
save this hollow heart of mine.

In every night sky
I need your shrine.
The rituals of your religion
are my sole source of delirium.

TWO STARS

Two stars shine bright
two lovers sky high
parted by the daylight
ushered together by the night

Two stars shine bright
but one sparkles a little more
you're the better half
the one with a purer soul

Two stars shine bright
whispering secrets untold
our morning masks are ruses
sleight of hand for the abuses

Two stars shine bright
two lovers embrace
parted by the daylight
ushered together by the night again

Two stars shine bright
one chides like a child
I hope you forgive me
these harmless sins of mine

Two stars shine bright
burning hotter than the sun

dampen this love quick
else bad luck shall come

Two stars shine bright
two lovers share a kiss
parted by the break of light
ushered back together at dusk again

Two stars shined bright
but one starts flickering away
our hands are bound
in the wavering vines of fate

Two stars no more
but the soul shines bright
one star didn't make it
but the heart survived

Two stars once shone
two lovers met in the sky
parted every day
ushered home together at night.

THE LOVERS COURT

I met a man in Bengaluru
a spry old fellow indeed,
he may have looked ancient
but his smile was childishly sweet.

He was skipping down the street
practically giddy with joy,
greeting every soul around
with a cheerful 'morning' lullaby.

As he turned to me I asked,
'Why so exuberant in your glee?
I've never seen such happiness
sweep through a man almost deceased'

His laughter rumbled low
that smile grew wider still,
'A joyous day it is, my friend
I've traded my wife in for a young misses'

I was ill prepared for such idiocy
unable to conjure a thought
so I naturally threw a curse out loud
but what followed next was unforgettable

'Don't judge others boy
especially when you don't understand

you know nought but what you've just seen
but there's a universe inside every man'

'It's easy to judge
you only know of this moment
it's the journey that shapes us
but how could you know it if we've just met?'

'These may just the scoldings
of the deliriously old,
you may think I know nothing
though I've outlived your granddaddies, boiyo'

I mumbled my apologies
and just like that he forgave,
'So what was I telling you?
Ah, yes, the Lovers Court is open again'

Before I could ask
he rumbled on in response,
'It's where lovers quarrel
to prove who was ultimately at fault'

'I spent half a century searching
for a wife who ran away
I finally found her at some market
she'd married my best mate'

'They're as happy as could be
I'd be blind not to see it

so I wished them the very best...
then I sued her cheating ass'

'The Lovers Court is ancient
it's only objective to adjudicate
upon every just claim
in any romantic engagement'

'No one knows of its origin,
presided by changing faces.
There's magic in those hallways,
justice in every sacred step.'

'Let all arguments be put before it
parties are given their just dues
it doesn't discriminate on any ground
a temple of justice for all lovers scorned'

'When a broken heart laments
over moments wasted away
when such scorned hearts on every corner
drowning in collective, cruel pain'

'That's when the court opens again
to ease the grief of hearts gravely maimed
to relieve this recurring hurt in humanity
only to shut suddenly without warning'

'Just knock when it opens next
find a way to survive until it leads you to itself

that's the test, the price you must pay
fight on until life feels you've learnt from past mistakes'

'The Court can give you back lost time
or settle the matter any which way.
Me? I got back all those years I wasted
and was matched to a woman who was suing her husband'

'So I apologise for my joy
if such a thing should even exists
look there comes Ava!'
And he pointed near my ear.

I could barely recognise him then
he'd grown younger with every breath.
Now stood a young man not unlike me
kissing a woman from some divine dream.

I did reflect briefly
on an amusing thought,
never could I have imagined
that this is how my day would start.

'I'm leaving now boy
don't forget what I've said.
if you're ever wronged in love
don't forever cry in piteous pain'

'Plead to the Lovers Court
beg before it if you must

don't worry about the heartbreak
it's all worth it in the end.'

He gave me a final wave,
I said my 'goodbye' and turned
How could such a thing exist?
It sounded like a children's book.

Yet here was proof
that old man had just morphed before me,
many years later though
I was proved wrong by its existence.

All good things must well and truly end
if they didn't then we wouldn't treasure them,
but if you ever find yourself in heartbroken despair
just knock on the door of the old Lovers Court.

WOLVES OF WILD HEARTS

I've long held this belief
two wolves fight inside me
to the victor go the spoils
control over these weary toils.

One wolf jet black
basked in deeds of the damned.
The other snow white
loyal and regally right.

A constant struggle
this war eternal
Which wolf should I feed?
Which one must die in hunger?

One wolf will take over
only that do I decide
what happens thereafter
are not my conscious crimes.

So long have I fed
the dark wolf of death
that misery and destruction
are forever my sins to wear.

But how is it you feed
this wolf white and bruised?

Why do I feel this sudden need
to try and be pure?

So now I only feed
this white wolf of love
I've become the better
of the two wolves of wild hearts.

The Gen-Y POET

J. Valentine

Did you like the book?

Email your questions, experiences, and suggestions to the author at

j.valentine.7@outlook.com

Crowd-Funders

(names listed alphabetically)

- Aadamvir Singh
- Aathif Jalal
- Amita Poyrekar
- Amita Thakur
- Anan Banka
- Anita Makhija
- Anju Taneja
- Anway Pramanik
- Arun Katiyar
- Asha Jolson
- Asha Kannan
- Asha Khandpur
- Ashita Shah
- Avanija Reddy
- Bhanu Thambi
- Deepti Mohan
- Devender Taneja
- Devyani Chaudhury
- Dhiraj Nandwani
- Dipannita Pathak
- Divya Krishnan
- Dr. Kiran K Kamat
- Dr. Jawahar Joshi
- Geetha Prem
- Himanshu Arora
- Hina Dedhia
- Hiten Dadia
- Indira Bharadwaj
- Isha Sagar
- Ishaana Aiyanna
- Ishneet Arora
- Jagdish Shettigar
- Joaquim Mario Pereira
- Kala Devarajan
- Kalpana Wadhwa
- Kalyani Tembe
- Kavita Rode
- Ketan Agarwal
- Kunal shah
- Kusum Hegde
- Laya Rikkamalle
- Mahek Lulla
- Mahesh Mahadeo
- Manoj Soni
- Maria Fernando
- Mathangi Sampath
- Meera Shah
- Monika Mangsule
- Mrudula Vartak
- Narendra Rathod
- Nayanatara Shankar
- Nila Rao
- Nimitt Dixit
- Nimrata Bhatia
- Pratima Singh
- Pratul Agarwal
- Preet Arya
- Preety Thapar
- Raghuram Kasavaraju
- Rajesh Saini
- Rakesh Sarawgi
- Ram Ramakrishnan
- Renu Warrier
- Resham Bhatia
- Riddhi Dabhi
- Rosy Singh
- Sanjay Singh
- Sapna Shettigar
- Satish Padmanabhan

- Sayali Pawar
- Shambhavi Singh
- Sharmila Prabhu
- Shashi Singh
- Shilpa Gupta
- Shradha Bakshi
- Siddhant Chandra
- Simran Senani
- Sonal Mehta
- Sonia Bhatia
- Stany Dsouza
- Subhash Bilore
- Sudhir Naik
- Suman Sodeshi
- Swamidas Kondle
- Swarleen kochhar
- Taniya Chauhan
- Theekshna Amin
- Utkarsh Jain
- Vandana Bagga
- Veena Bhandary
- Vijay Bharadwaj
- Vijay Degalahal
- Vijay Jadhav
- Vinod Rajpal
- Vivek K R